Jimb stowaway, but Captain Roger allowed him to join the crew as ship's boy

Flashfork, ship's cook. He is no master chef but the crew rarely complain; he's a hot-tempered man, armed with a cutlass and a rolling pin!

Anne, the daughter of Bessie, landlady at the inn on Pirate Island. She is a fearless pirate and loves to take part in Darkshark's adventures whenever she can

Spinoza, the mischievous ship's monkey and **Popsy**, Captain Roger's faithful and very talkative parrot

The Tropical Sea is a great place for adventure. There are pirates, pirate ships and pirate adventures, with Captain Roger, Bo'sun Will and the crew of the Darkshark constantly pitting their wits against their arch enemies, Captain Foul and the crew of the Barracuda.

British Library Cataloguing in Publication Data

Grant, John *1930-*
    Adventure on Shark Island.
    I. Title   II. Davis, Jon   III. Series
    823.914[J]
    ISBN 0-7214-1345-5

First edition

Published by Ladybird Books Ltd Loughborough Leicestershire UK
Ladybird Books Inc Auburn Maine 04210 USA

® LEGO is a registered trademark belonging to the LEGO Group and is used here
   by special permission.
© LEGO GROUP MCMXC
© LADYBIRD BOOKS LTD MCMXC

Printed in England (3)

Adventure on Shark Island

by JOHN GRANT
illustrated by JON DAVIS

Ladybird Books

One morning, *Darkshark* dropped anchor off Pirates' Nest. Captain Roger sat in his cabin writing in the ship's ledger. He and Will were adding up the takings from the latest voyage. It came to exactly three doubloons.

"And two of those are fake," said Will.

"So, that's all we have to show for a month at sea," sighed the Captain, miserably. "Not a single treasure ship! No cargo ships! Only one miserable schooner! Not worth the powder and shot!"

He put the one good doubloon in his pocket and he went ashore followed by Will and the rest of the crew.

In the "Keg and Cutlass" Roger put his one doubloon on the counter. "A bottle of rum and twelve straws, please, Bessie," he said.

At that moment the door of the inn burst open and in came Captain Foul and the crew of the *Barracuda*. They were laughing and shouting.

"Best voyage we've had in years!" bellowed Foul. "Bessie! Bring roast beef for me and my men! Roast potatoes! Vegetables! And jam roly-poly to follow!"

He looked across at the crew of *Darkshark* huddled around their bottle of rum. "Call yourselves pirates!" he jeered. "Maybe we should give you some lessons!"

"We don't need lessons!" cried Captain Roger. "Especially from the likes of you!" And he drew his cutlass and leapt across the table. The others followed, and in a moment chaos reigned.

Bessie grabbed the blunderbuss she kept behind the bar and fired it in the air. Plaster fell from the ceiling, but the pirates didn't stop fighting.

Then Anne had an idea. She slipped out of the back door of the inn and ran to the front. Then she burst through the door shouting, "*Barracuda*'s under attack!

They're looting the hold! The sails are on fire! Quick!"

The crew of *Darkshark* suddenly found themselves alone, as Foul and his crew fled to their ship.

When Captain Foul realised that they had been tricked, he was furious. "It was that meddling female from the *Darkshark*," he snarled. "We've got to teach her a lesson!"

A day or two later Anne was strolling along the quay with Popsy on her shoulder. She didn't notice the cargo net spread out in front of her, and next moment she and Popsy were hoisted, tangled in the net, on board *Barracuda*. It took most of the crew to drag Anne, fighting, from the net. Then they pushed her into a barrel with some food and water and hoisted the barrel to the masthead. Anne was a prisoner.

"Well done, men!" cried Foul. "Raise the anchor. We'll sail on the next tide."

The crew of *Darkshark* searched high and low as soon as they realised that Anne was missing. And Popsy was missing too. But not for long. Tired and bedraggled, she fluttered over Pirate Island and flopped down on *Darkshark*'s deck. There was a note tied to her leg.

We've got Anne,
Bring one thousand doubloons to Shark Island and you can have her back in one piece... or else!   FOUL

"He wants a ransom!" cried Captain Roger. "We don't pay ransoms!"

"We can't anyway," said Rummy. "We've only got two fake doubloons!"

"Then we'll rescue Anne!" cried Will. "Right, Captain?"

Provisioned by Bessie, *Darkshark* set sail. Two days later the look-out sighted land, and by sunset *Darkshark* was at anchor off Shark Island.

As the moon rose, Will and Jimbo rowed across to the island to search for Anne. They hauled the boat up the beach, then pushed their way through dark jungle where wild creatures rustled and screeched and growled in the undergrowth.

Beyond the jungle was a sandy beach. And beyond that *Barracuda* lay at anchor.

In the bright moonlight every detail of the ship was clear, and through his telescope, Will could make out a barrel lashed near the top of the mainmast. As he looked, a familiar head wearing a blue scarf appeared above the barrel's rim.

They had found Anne!

Back aboard *Darkshark* Will explained the situation to Captain Roger.

"The way they have Anne imprisoned, she can't get down and a person couldn't get up to her. But a monkey could. Where's Spinoza?"

At the mention of his name Spinoza came running from the quarterdeck. Jimbo took a bag of nuts from his pocket

and fed some to the monkey as Will explained his plan.

"Tomorrow, after dark, Spinoza, Jimbo and I will sail a small boat round to where *Barracuda* is anchored. Spinoza will climb up to Anne with a line of strong rope. Anne will tie the rope to the mast... and the rest should be easy!"

"How will Anne know what to do?" asked Captain Roger.

"Popsy will take a message," said Will. And he sat down with the parrot on his wrist. "Say after me, Popsy, 'WILL IS COMING, STAND BY.'"

By lunchtime Popsy had it right. Will pointed across the island. "Find Anne, Popsy!" he cried.

As darkness fell, Will, Jimbo and
Spinoza set off, steering a careful course
through the rocks and shallows close to
the tip of Shark Island.

There were a few lights on *Barracuda*, but there was no one on deck to see the small boat glide alongside.

Carrying the length of rope, Spinoza scrambled up the rigging. He reached the barrel, and Anne took the rope and secured it to the mast. A moment later she was out of the barrel and sliding down to join Will and Jimbo.

"Where's Spinoza?" whispered Jimbo.

The monkey was nowhere to be seen.

Spinoza was in no hurry to leave. Here was a new ship to explore. He scampered along the deck to a lighted doorway. It was Captain Foul's cabin. And the Captain was busy at one of his favourite occupations – counting his money. Little piles of gold coins lay on

the table. With a happy smile he put all the money into a small cloth bag and drew the string tight. The bag was very like the one in which Jimbo kept Spinoza's favourite nuts. Quick as a flash, the monkey darted into the cabin and seized the bag!

"Stop thief!" bellowed Captain Foul. "Catch that monkey!"

Spinoza ran towards the bow of the ship. The bag was heavy – really *too* heavy, so he decided to hide it, and thrust it down the barrel of one of the bow-chaser cannons. Then he leapt overboard to join Jimbo, Will and Anne.

Culverin spotted the boat. "The prisoner's getting away," he cried.

"After them!" cried Foul.

But already the dinghy was skimming across the moonlit water.

Will looked back. *Barracuda* was beginning to gain on them. Now was the time for quick thinking. He steered the dinghy close to shore. *Barracuda* followed – right among the rocks and shallows at the tip of the island.

With a bump and a
crunch *Barracuda* ran
aground.

"Don't let them get
away!" screamed
Foul. "Sink them!"

Culverin ran up to
the forecastle and fired one of the bow-
chaser cannons.

Will, Anne and Jimbo ducked as cannon shot splashed into the sea. Then something hit the sail with a thump... and gold coins clinked and jingled about their ears and into the bottom of the boat.

"Fancy," said Anne, "Captain Foul has sent a farewell present!" And they all filled their pockets with the money. Spinoza found the empty bag and was disappointed that there were no nuts!

Captain Roger and the crew cheered when Will and Jimbo arrived back with Anne. They cheered even louder when they saw the money.

"Make sail!" cried Roger. "Next stop Pirates' Nest and the 'Keg and Cutlass'. Then it's roast beef and jam roly-poly all round... double helpings!"

THE TREASURE ISLANDS

JOHN SILVER ISLAND

Darkshark, Captain Roger's ship

THE TROPICAL S

FORT SABRE

PORT ROYAL

SABATINA

FENZANCE

PIRATE'S HAT ISLAND

SHARK ISLAND

ISLAND OF FOG